I Love Ramadan

أنا أحب رمضان

Copyright © 2018 by Taymaa Salhah. All rights reserved.
جميع الحقوق محفوظة | تيماء صالحة © ٢٠١٨
ISBN: 978-1-7751528-0-4

I am very happy! Tomorrow is the first day of the month of Ramadan.

أنا فرحان! غداً هو أول أيام شهر رمضان.

Ramadan is a special month. Quran was revealed in Ramadan.

شهر رمضان شهر مميز، أنزل فيه القرآن.

Ramadan is the month of fasting. When I fast, I do not eat nor drink from dawn to sunset.

شهر رمضان هو شهر الصيام. عندما أصوم، لا آكل و لا أشرب من طلوع الفجر إلى غروب الشمس.

During Ramadan, I wake up before dawn for suhur.

أستيقظ في رمضان قبل طلوع الفجر لأتناول السحور.

I finish my meal before athan alfajr and fast until sunset.

أكمل طعامي قبل آذان الفجر و أصوم حتى غروب الشمس.

I read Quran and recite tasbeeh frequently.
"Glory be to Allah. Praise be to Allah.
There is no God but Allah. Allah is the greatest."

أكثر من قراءة القرآن و التسبيح.

"سبحان الله، الحمد لله، لا إله إلا الله، و الله أكبر."

When I hear athan almaghreb, I recite dua and break my
fast with my family.
عند سماع آذان المغرب، أدعو الله و أتناول وجبة الإفطار مع أسرتي.

At night, I go to the mosque for taraweeh prayer.

عند حلول الليل، أذهب إلى المسجد لأصلي التراويح.

When Ramadan is over, we celebrate Eid Elfitr!

عند انتهاء شهر رمضان، نحتفل بعيد الفطر!

CPSIA information can be obtained
at www.ICGtesting.com
Printed in the USA
BVHW021734190822
645023BV00006B/133